D0480808

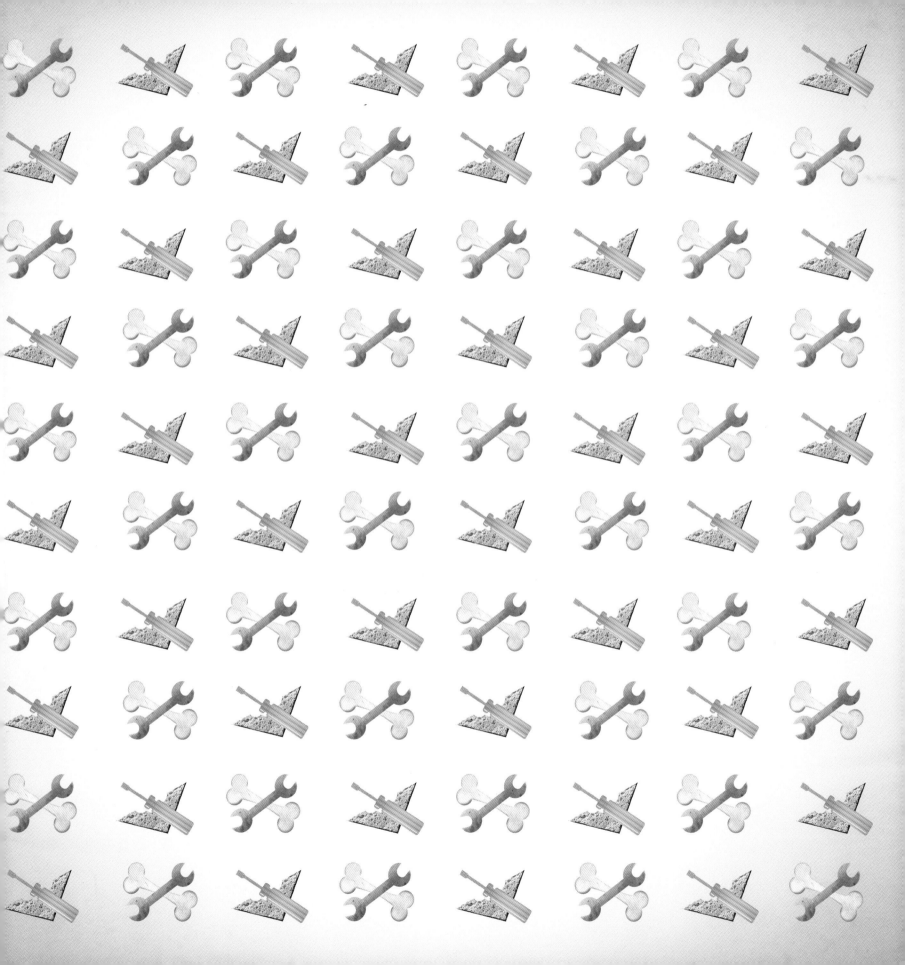

IMAGINE THAT™

Licensed exclusively to Imagine That Publishing Ltd
Tide Mill Way, Woodbridge, Suffolk, IP12 1AP, UK
www.imaginethat.com
Copyright © 2019 Gary Boller
All rights reserved
0 2 4 6 8 9 7 5 3 1
Manufactured in China

Written and illustrated by Gary Boller

All rights reserved. No part of this publication may be reproduced, stored in a retrieval system, or
transmitted in any form or by any means, electronic, mechanical, photocopying, recording or otherwise,
without the prior written permission of the publisher. Neither this book nor any part or any of the
illustrations, photographs or reproductions contained in it shall be sold or disposed of otherwise than as
a complete book, and any unauthorised sale of such part illustration, photograph or reproduction shall be
deemed to be a breach of the publisher's copyright.

ISBN 978-1-78958-589-6

A catalogue record for this book is available from the British Library

ROVER'S Scrapyard

WRITTEN AND ILLUSTRATED BY GARY BOLLER

This is Rover. He's a yappy, happy dog! He's happy because he has a scrapyard full of old, broken things.

Rover loves old, broken things – even his favourite old jumper is full of holes!

Every morning, Rover fetches his toolbox and gets to work. There's always another old car to take apart!

OFFICE

TOOLS

Rover doesn't like throwing stuff away. He likes collecting all the old bits of cars and machinery that people have dumped.

Rover's pet rat, Morris, helps.
They pile up the old cars with
Rover's crane. It's a good job
that the crane can reach up high!

DANGER! DOG AT WORK

'RIGHT! LET'S GET TO WORK, MORRIS,'

says Rover one morning. He grabs his biggest wrench and climbs up on to a rusty car.

He takes the doors off,

then he pops the glass out.

He lifts the engine up.

Finally, Rover rips the radio out. Morris helps him snip the wires.

SNIP!

TOOLS

'LUNCH BREAK!' shouts Rover.

Rover washes his hands, but he doesn't do it very well so his cheese sandwich gets a bit oily. He gives some to Morris who doesn't mind a bit.

While they eat,
Morris puts a record
on Rover's old-fashioned
jukebox. They both love
old-fashioned things.

Rover and Morris get back to work, and they soon have a pile of car parts.

Rover counts a headlamp, a gearbox, some wheels, four spark plugs and some money from down the back of the seats!

BOING!

Morris helps to put price tags on everything, then Rover puts them on the car shop shelves to sell.

But not everything is for sale. Rover sneaks some of the old bits through a secret door. He has a plan!

NO ENTRY!

DING! DING!

goes the door bell, and a smart lady customer comes in.

'Hello,' says Rover politely. 'How may I help you?'

I need a whatnot for a Winebago,' says the smart lady.

'Erm ... I'm afraid I don't have one of those,' says Rover hastily.

Another customer comes in.

'Have you got a discombobulator for a Datsun?' she asks.

'Erm ... no. I'm afraid I don't think I have one of those 'either!' says Rover, hiding one behind his back.

'I need a new skiddlyboo for a Suzuki,' says yet another customer.

'**NOPE!**' says Rover. 'Come back next week.'

TOOT!

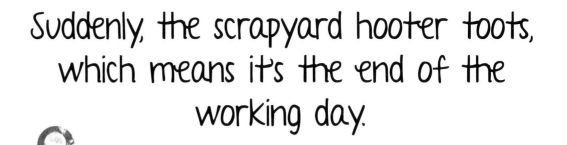

Suddenly, the scrapyard hooter toots,
which means it's the end of the
working day.

OFFICE

MORRIS

Rover closes his gate
and flips the sign over
to CLOSED.

CLOSED

Rover disappears through his secret door
with his bits and bobs.

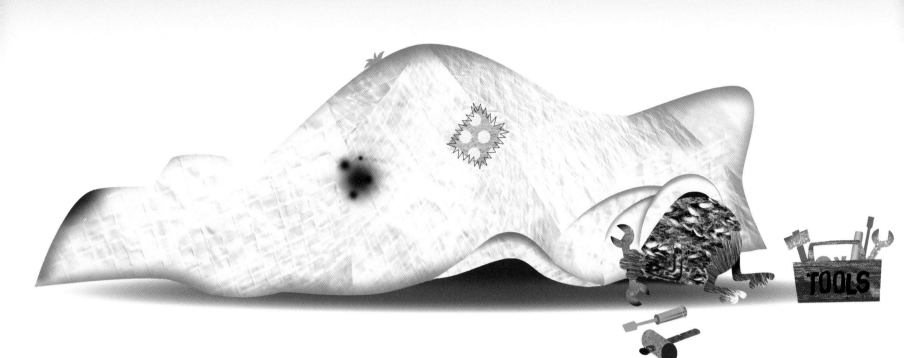

Outside, behind the scrapyard, is a dirty old sheet.
Rover lifts it up and crawls underneath.

There is a bang and a crash, a squeak
and a tappity tap. Then he calls,

'MORRIS!'

Morris scampers over. **'READY!'** says Rover and pulls off the sheet.

'TA-DAAA!' cries Rover.

There in the yard sits the
sparkliest, purplest, convertible,
super-duper, recycled,
flying Cadillac.

ROVER 1

Rover has used the steering wheel from a Ford, a bonnet from a Chevrolet, a skiddlyboo from a Suzuki, the discombobulator from a Datsun, wheels from a Hot Rod, a whatnot from a Winnebago and whirly blades from an old helicopter.

'TA-DAAA!'

Rover pops Morris into a special little seat.

'I need to open the gate for you,' squeaks Morris.

'No you don't,' says Rover, starting the engine which purrs like a big cat. 'We'll fly right over!'

BRUM BRUM

ROVER 1

He presses a button and the car takes off into the sky, flies over the gate and off over the city.

OFFICE

CLOSED

'We're going on holiday to the seaside!' cries Rover.

'Here, Morris. Have a whole cheese sandwich!'

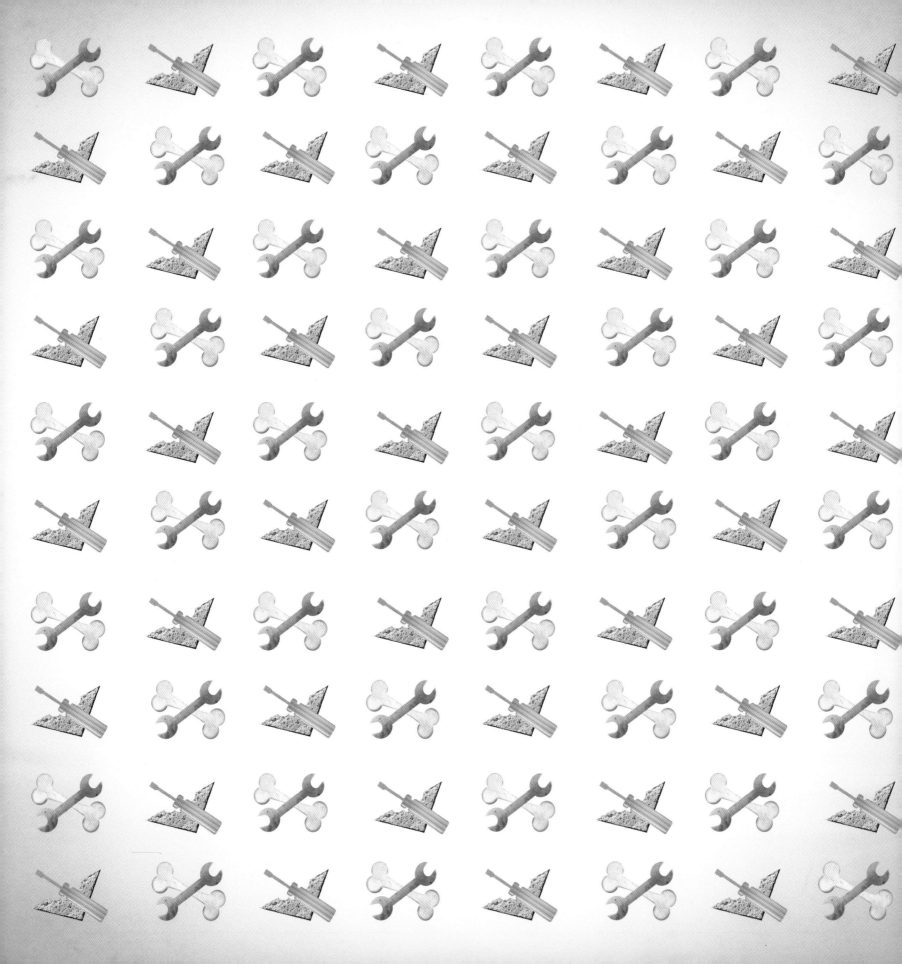

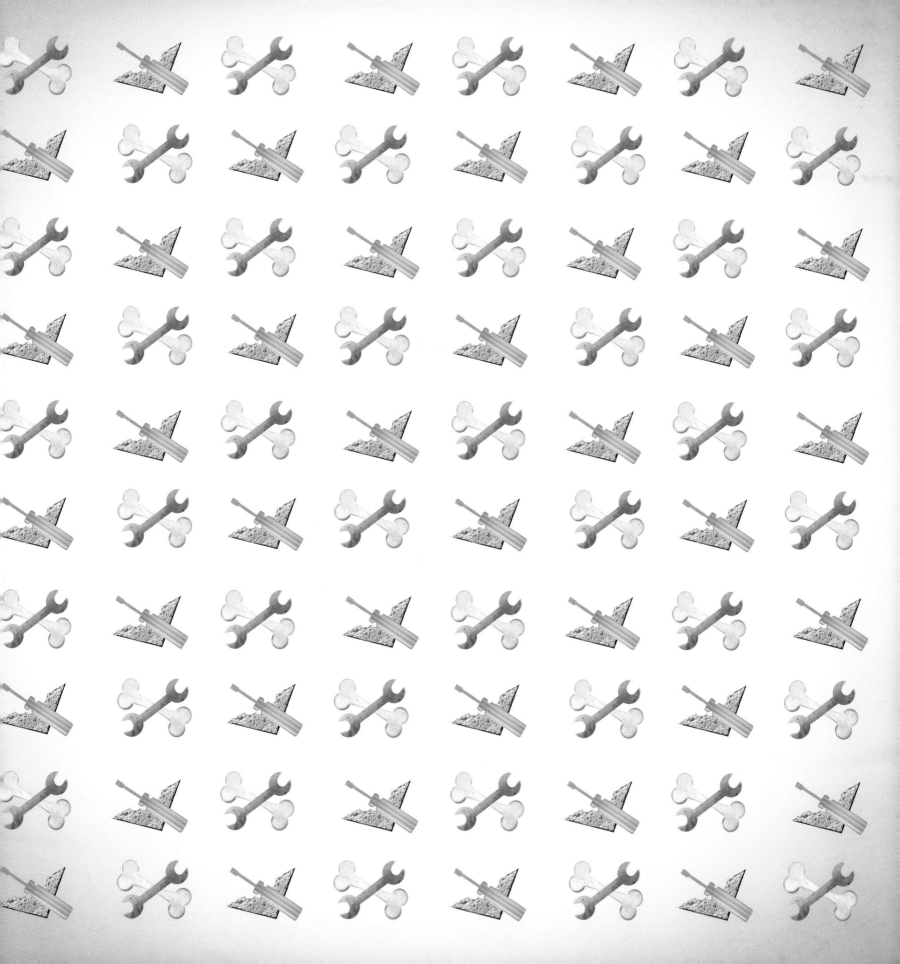